SUNNYSIDE
PRIMARY SCHOOL

Jake
in Danger

ANNETTE BUTTERWORTH

ILLUSTRATED BY
NICK BUTTERWORTH

Hodder
Children's
Books

a division of Hodder Headline plc

Text copyright © Annette Butterworth 1999
Illustrations copyright © Nick Butterworth 1999

First published in Great Britain in 1999
by Hodder Children's Books

A Catalogue record for this book is available from the British Library

ISBN 0 340 73309 8

Printed and bound in Great Britain by
Mackays of Chatham plc, Chatham, Kent

Hodder Children's Books
a division of Hodder Headline plc
338 Euston Road, London NW1 3BH

For
Charlie Fancourt,
One time fishmonger,
Sometimes bowler,
Always larger than life
And a great dad.

Chapter One

Jake was fed up.

Usually, he loved going for walks in the local park with his friend, Sam.

Usually, he was the star attraction with the other dogs. Holly, the Rough Collie, and Charles, the Irish Wolfhound, thought he was great fun. He played football like no other dog they knew. He could head the ball, then trap it with his legs and dribble it back along the ground, from any distance, in no time at all. Jake was the cleverest and the bravest of them all. He was every dog's favourite.

Usually.

But now a new dog had arrived in the neighbourhood, an Afghan Hound called Boris. He was extremely handsome with long flowing hair. He could run like the wind and could easily outrun any dog in the park, including Jake.

Boris told wonderful tales of foreign lands where he had lived. He talked about places far away, of different animals and smells. His owner had even taken him hunting from time to time and Boris had helped catch moose and deer.

"Not very nice for the moose and deer," Jake thought.

The other dogs were impressed. While Boris was around, no other dog got any attention, including Jake, and he wasn't used to this at all.

For the first time in his life, Jake felt jealous. And he didn't like it.

He tried to talk to his best friend, Holly, about it. She lived next door to Jake.

Holly told Jake that he was just being silly. Of course everybody still liked him, but really, Boris was so interesting.

So even Holly was impressed by Boris. And Jake was fed up.

Chapter Two

Jake's friend, Sam, was an old man whose garden backed onto Jake's. Through Jake, Sam had made friends with Jake's owners, Mr and Mrs Foster. Sam took Jake for walks in the local park, twice a day, weather permitting.

The summer was over now and the

leaves on the trees were changing colour, ready to drop to the ground. It was Sam's favourite time of year. He liked the colours of the trees, especially the vivid red of the maples.

One morning, when Sam arrived to take Jake for his walk, Mrs Foster had some news for him.

"Do you know the old man, Mr Wood, who lives in the big house next to the park, Sam?" she asked.

"He has lots of animals living with him, doesn't he? Some unusual animals, I've heard," said Sam.

"Yes," replied Mrs Foster. "Well, he's quite ill and can't look after himself. He's got to go into a home, so they need to do something with all his animals. Nobody seems to know how many he has or what they all are. Someone said that he has even got an alligator in there! Certainly, he has got five parrots because I've been told they need to rehouse them. The trouble is, Mr Wood doesn't want them to go into a zoo and he wants the parrots kept together."

"Well," Sam said, "I would be willing to take one, but what would I do with five parrots?"

"I don't think anyone will want five parrots. Apparently one of them can talk but I think it can only say 'clear off'. Not very friendly! It must be used to hearing Mr Wood," Mrs Foster laughed.

When Sam and Jake arrived at the park, Holly and her owner, Mrs Thirkettle, and Charles with his owner, Mr Grant, were already there. Jake was disappointed to see Boris and his owner, Mrs Baker, arriving as well.

As the dogs trotted together through the park, Boris talked non-stop about

Canada, another place where he had lived. They had reached a big mound in the ground which was covered in grass and bushes. There seemed to be a small hole in the side of the mound. Boris stopped talking about Canada to ask if anybody knew what it was.

Jake knew. He'd been through the hole into the mound many times.

He started to explain that inside the mound was an underground cave, very dark and damp. He had heard Mrs Thirkettle telling Sam something about it. She said it used to be an ice house. Ice was stored inside it and the ice was used to keep food cold and fresh, before people had fridges. Jake told Boris that now the hole was a great place to explore.

But Boris wasn't listening any more. He heard the word ice and carried on talking about Canada and how icy it was there and how he had once caught and killed a hare in the ice.

Jake wasn't used to dogs ignoring or interrupting him before he had finished. He was astonished.

The ice house was one of Jake's special places in the park. He liked to go inside to check it out whenever he could.

There were only a few old tools in there and the odd mouse, but for Jake, it was a secret place, hidden away from prying eyes. It was special. Jake felt quite hurt that Boris didn't even let him finish his tale.

The other dogs ran off towards the lake, listening to Boris's stories, leaving Jake alone, next to the ice house.

"That Boris," Jake thought. "He's too full of himself. He's got too much to say." Then he trotted slowly towards the lake, gradually catching up with the others.

When Jake arrived at the lake, the other dogs had already made a horrible discovery. There was an injured gosling lying by the side of the lake.

Sam counted the goslings and sighed. "One has disappeared. And this one is dead I'm afraid. Foxes, I suppose," he said.

"Just a minute," said Mr Grant. "This footprint in the mud is too big for a fox. It's more like a big dog or even a wild cat!"

"Good gracious!" said Mrs Thirkettle. "I've heard about that sort of thing. In my newspaper there was a story about a puma that escaped from a zoo. It attacked several little dogs before it was captured. I hope we haven't got something like that here!"

The dogs looked at one another. They hoped so too. But there was definitely something prowling about the park and it had killed the goslings.

Jake looked again at the paw print. Somehow, it didn't look like the shape of a cat's print, even a big one. It reminded him of somebody else's paw print.

Jake looked suspiciously at Boris.

"I don't trust him," Jake thought. "He

lives right next to the park and could sneak in here any time. He needs watching."

Chapter Three

The next day, Sam was having a cup of tea with the Fosters before he went on his morning walk with Jake. They were chatting about Mr Wood, the old man with the unusual animals.

Mr Wood was getting more and more upset. He couldn't part with his "babies", as he called them, unless he knew they would all be together and well looked after.

Mrs Foster was very worried about him. "I think he might do something silly if he thinks the animals will be locked up," she said. "He seemed very agitated when I spoke to him yesterday, which is not very good for him."

"They need to find a wildlife park or farm or something that will take all the animals," Mr Foster said.

"Yes," Sam agreed. "Otherwise, who would have space for five parrots? Where does Mr Wood keep them all?"

"They fly around the house," replied Mrs Foster. "And make a terrible mess!"

"Well, we must go to the park now Jake and let you fly around that," Sam said and he put Jake's lead on him.

"At last!" Jake thought.

When they arrived at the park, Jake ran down to the lake to chase the ducks into the water. There were lots of fallen leaves lying by the water's edge, so, at first, Jake didn't notice the duck, but he did see mounds of feathers strewn around the pathway. Then he saw it.

Lying by the lake, with its beak in the water, was a poor old mallard duck. It was dead. And Jake could see it had been half-eaten. There were footprints in the mud, the same shape as before.

"Boris!" thought Jake. And then he looked at his own feet and noticed that they looked similar to the paw prints. "They must be a dog's prints. And I think I know which dog! Why doesn't anybody else look at them and see that?"

Jake ran back to Sam to find him talking with Mrs Thirkettle. She already knew about the duck.

"Do you think it could be a puma, Sam?" Mrs Thirkettle said. "I'm so worried for Holly. She's too good-natured to stick up for herself. She wouldn't fight anything, certainly not a fierce big cat."

"Don't worry," Sam said, "I'm sure Holly will be all right. This creature, whatever it is, hunts at night. Besides, Holly is a lot bigger than a duck!"

Holly didn't seem too sure. She trotted along with Jake, telling him that she wasn't very brave, not like Jake.

Jake told Holly to stick with him, that he would look after her. Then he paused. Should he tell Holly what he thought about Boris? It might stop her worrying about a puma.

He decided he would. He began to tell Holly about his suspicions. He thought it was much more likely that it was Boris who was killing the birds.

Holly was astonished. Surely Boris wouldn't do a thing like that. It was too horrible to think about. He didn't need to kill the birds. He was well fed at home.

Jake reminded her of Boris's hunting tales. Sometimes dogs enjoyed hunting so much that they didn't know when to stop.

Holly was forced to admit that, perhaps, Jake could be right.

The two dogs trotted on until they reached the ice house. Holly never followed Jake into the ice house. She didn't like the place. Jake was about to go down into it, when he caught the whiff of a strange smell. It was a very strong, new smell and it was coming out of the hole. Jake was excited.

"Good," he thought. "Something new." But just as he was going into the hole, Sam called out. Jake tried to ignore him but Sam's call was insistent.

Reluctantly, Jake ran back to Sam, leaving the ice house and its new smell unexplored.

* * *

As it turned out, Jake didn't get another opportunity to explore the ice house. Another duck disappeared from the lake, leaving only its feathers. Then the park authorities decided to act. They were not taking any risks, so dog owners were told to keep their dogs on a lead in the park. No more running around loose.

For Jake, this meant no more football. This was very bad news. He loved to play football and he had too much energy to stay on a lead.

Sam and the Fosters were very disappointed. They had a big problem. How were they going to get rid of all Jake's energy? Unless the killer was found, the dogs would have to stay on their leads in the park. For a big, energetic dog like Jake, this would be awful.

Chapter Four

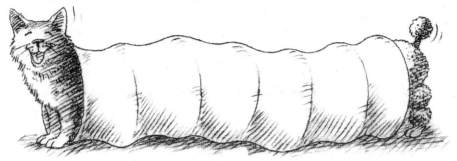

Mrs Foster thought she might have found a way of using up some of Jake's energy. A local dog club ran classes for dogs performing all sorts of tricks. They called it agility.

There were lots of different things to do at the agility classes. There were jumps for them to jump over, plastic tunnels for them to run through, trapezes for them to climb up and down and platforms to jump on. It was like an adventure playground. Dogs had to be agile and fast, and to pay attention to their owners.

Mrs Foster thought it might be just

right for Jake. She and Sam decided to take Jake along to give it a try.

Sam was looking forward to the evening. He didn't like keeping Jake on his lead in the park and today they had been twice. Jake was still full of energy, even after the second walk. Tonight would be different. Agility would give Jake a chance to shine.

When they arrived at the class, the expert dogs were already there, practising for a display. One of the events involved a set of poles spread out in a straight line. The dogs would try to run in and out of them as fast as they could, without missing any.

Jake watched them, weaving through the poles.

"I could easily do that," he thought. "Simple."

Soon the expert dogs had finished and

it was time for the beginners, like Jake, to have a go.

Beginner dogs were kept on their leads to start with, so that they could be helped and guided more easily.

Mrs Foster and Jake were shown a long line of poles and an instructor told Mrs Foster what to do. Jake watched the other dogs and quickly learnt how to weave in and out. Mrs Foster made him walk slowly through the poles.

Jake didn't think much of this. He knew he could go much faster.

Mrs Foster was pleased with their first attempt. Jake seemed to understand what to do, he had done quite well, so Mrs Foster decided to try again. She started to walk slowly through the poles.

But Jake had other ideas. He raced at the poles, knocking most of them down and dragging Mrs Foster along behind him. Then Jake's lead got stuck around one of the poles and all of them fell over, knocking Mrs Foster down to the floor. She ended up in a heap with Jake and the poles lying on top of her.

"Oh dear," Sam said, helping Mrs Foster up off the floor. "Are you all right?"

"Yes, I think so," Mrs Foster said, shakily, and she checked herself over. "No broken bones. But I might have known. I thought things were going too smoothly."

"Let me try Jake with something else," Sam said. He took Jake's lead and tried to calm him down. Then he led Jake over to a platform that looked like a very high table. Other dogs jumped onto it and stayed there for a few seconds then jumped off.

"Simple," thought Jake.

Sam had to take Jake's lead off for this exercise. He led Jake over to the high table, sat him down, took his lead off and then told him to jump up onto the table. Jake took a flying leap at the platform, jumped much too far, right over it, and landed on a little poodle dog on the other side. The poor poodle was very shocked and so was its owner.

Sam apologised to them, and took Jake back to Mrs Foster.

"Perhaps we'll give him one more try," Mrs Foster said. "It looks as though he prefers jumping over things to landing on them! They've set out some high jumps over there, let's try them."

Sam took Jake over to the jumps and waited in line ready to have a go.

Jake tried the first jump and found it easy. The second one was higher and Jake still found it easy.

"I like this," Jake thought. He then jumped over a third and a fourth jump. But he didn't stop there. Sam watched in astonishment as Jake went jumping all round the hall. He jumped over dogs, people, chairs, everything in his path. Jake was so excited he got carried away. The hall was in uproar with dogs and people trying to get out of Jake's way.

Eventually, the agility organiser caught Jake and put a lead on him. He led him over to Mrs Foster and Sam.

"I'm sorry," he said, "your dog is very agile and very fast. But he's too enthusiastic! I don't think we can cope with him."

Sam, Mrs Foster and Jake went home feeling very fed up.

Jake was extremely disappointed. He had really enjoyed himself and thought he had done very well. He had been faster than any other dog and he had jumped more than any other dog. He was sure with a bit more practise, he could improve his performance. But the agility instructor didn't agree. He asked Mrs Foster not to bring Jake again.

Chapter Five

Sam was worried about Jake. Jake needed lots of exercise, he needed to run free. After the agility classes, Jake just wasn't himself. His usual bouncy stride had gone. He no longer seemed interested in going for a walk.

Jake was bored. He started to chew his box and even had a chew at the mat in the hall. He hated being stuck on the lead all the time. If he wasn't allowed to roam around the park, discovering things for himself, he didn't see much point in going. He certainly wasn't interested in just walking.

Then Sam had an idea. He decided to take Jake to the park, after dark, when it was locked up for the day. He knew a side gate which the park keeper always left unlocked. He would let Jake run off the lead and no one would know.

One evening, Sam and Jake sneaked through the gate. It was very misty and Sam was glad. It would be even harder for anyone to see Jake running around off the lead.

Jake was thrilled. He rushed every-where, checking everything. He was so pleased to be free at last. When he ran back to Sam, he almost knocked him over, he was so full of beans.

"Steady old thing. This mist is making the path slippery. You'll knock me over!" Sam said.

Jake ran off once more. Suddenly, as he got near the lake, Jake heard a terrible piercing cry and a great flapping of wings. He ran down to the water's edge and just caught a glimpse of a shadowy shape through the mist, slinking away into the bushes. But Jake had seen enough to know it was a four-legged beast. It was short haired. And it wasn't Boris. Maybe it was a wild cat.

Jake looked at a white heap lying by the lake. It was the body of a swan. It was covered in blood. Jake sniffed at the swan, trying to smell the scent of the beast that had killed it. It was a strange scent, but somehow familiar to Jake. He had smelt the same scent when he was at the ice house the last time, just before Sam had called him away.

"It must be living in the ice house!" Jake thought. "And it must be very fierce to be able to kill a swan. They are so strong."

Jake sniffed closely again at the swan, but as he did, he got some of the swan's blood on his muzzle.

Jake wasn't the only one who had heard the swan's cries. A lady living in a house close to the lake had been so frightened by the noise that she had called the police. Straight away, a policeman had been sent to the park to find out what was happening.

The policeman arrived at the lakeside at the same time as Sam. They found Jake standing next to a dead swan. Then they saw the blood on his muzzle. The policeman turned to Sam.

"Is this your dog?"

Sam was silent.

"Killing a swan is a very serious business. All the swans in the land belong to the Queen. I shall have to file a report about this."

Sam was white with shock. He just couldn't believe Jake had killed the swan. "What will happen?" he asked, shakily.

"That will be up to the magistrates

34

court to decide. The magistrate could order the dog to be destroyed. Sometimes, that's the only way to stop a killer dog," the policeman said.

"There must be some mistake," Sam said. "Jake wouldn't kill anything."

"Well, it doesn't look that way to me," the policeman said. "And I think you'll have a hard job proving otherwise. Please report to me at the police station tomorrow morning so that I can write my report. Then we'll have to see what the magistrate has to say. As for this dog, you must keep him on a lead in public places and firmly under control until the case comes up in court. Otherwise I shall have to take him into police custody."

Sam was stunned. He put Jake's lead on him and tried to clean the blood off his muzzle with his handkerchief.

Jake was angry. He hadn't killed the

swan and, what's more, he thought he knew where the real killer was hiding. But now Jake would be watched so closely there would be no chance of his finding the beast.

If the real culprit wasn't found, Jake would be blamed. Sam hated to think what might happen to him then.

Chapter Six

When Sam and Jake arrived at the park the next morning, all the other dogs and their owners were discussing the events of the night before.

Jake wondered what they were saying. Did they believe that he had killed the swan? How could he convince his friends that he hadn't?

As Sam and Jake approached the little

band of friends, Mrs Thirkettle called, "Good morning, Sam. Terrible business about the swan. Whatever got into Jake?"

"Good morning," replied Sam. "I don't believe it was Jake. He wouldn't kill anything."

"I hope you're right," Mr Grant said. "But how are you going to prove it?"

Sam shrugged. He didn't know.

"It would be terrible if they find Jake guilty and order him to be taken way," Mrs Thirkettle said. "The magistrate could do that, couldn't he? Jake deserves better than that."

Jake stood as far away from the other dogs as his lead would allow him. He glanced at them, hoping they would accept him still as their friend, but he wasn't sure.

It was Holly who spoke to him first. She asked him what had happened with the swan. She also told him that all the dogs had agreed that they didn't believe Jake had killed it.

Jake was very relieved that his friends felt like this and he told them what had really happened. He was surprised to find that even Boris believed him. Jake thought that perhaps he had misjudged the Afghan. He felt ashamed that he'd been so unfriendly towards Boris and thought such horrible things about him. He told Holly that he had seen the creature in the mist and it definitely wasn't Boris. Holly was glad.

Jake told the dogs that he thought the creature was living in the ice house. Boris was particularly interested in this. He too had smelt a strange smell coming from it. It reminded him of Canada.

The dogs agreed on one thing. The beast, whatever it was, hunted at night.

Jake knew that unless the beast could be tempted out in the daytime, when people were in the park, nobody would discover it. And Jake would end up in the magistrates court.

Holly was shocked. Something had to be done. But what could the dogs do, when they were kept on leads in the park?

Suddenly the group of friends were interrupted by a loud squawking, coming from a big oak tree.

"Clear off! Clear off!" they heard.

The dogs and their owners looked up into the oak tree to see what was making the noise. High up in the branches, squawking away at a family of rooks, was a beautiful grey parrot.

"Clear off!" it squawked again. "Clear off!"

Sam laughed. It was one of Mr Wood's

parrots. It must have
escaped from his house.

"It'll be a hard job to
capture him," Sam said.

The parrot carried on
squawking, until, at
last, an animal
handler arrived in
the park, with a
cage.

"Clear off!"
repeated the parrot, but it
couldn't resist some fat juicy grapes that
were offered to it and the animal handler
finally got it into the cage.

"What will happen to it?" Sam asked
the man.

"I'm taking it back to Mr Wood. It got
out by mistake," the handler said. "But
soon they are all going to be moving on."

The little band carried on through the

park but all the dogs were quiet. They were all worried for Jake. Boris was particularly quiet, for him. He was thinking very hard.

Boris had a plan. If all the dogs worked together, they might be able to get the creature to leave the ice house. Together, they must trick the owners into letting go of one of the leads. Then the freed dog could run to the ice house and try to entice the creature out into the open. It could be very dangerous. Nobody knew what sort of creature it was. It had killed a swan easily. It would be more than a match for any dog.

The dogs were silent. They all wanted to help Jake. But who would dare?

For Jake, there was a simple answer. He would do it.

If the others could get Sam to let go of his lead, Jake would run to the ice house and confront the creature. He had nothing to lose.

The other dogs thought Jake was very brave. But was it the right thing to do?

Jake knew it was. Soon, he would be going to the magistrates court, and he might not come back. He would rather take his chance with the creature in the ice house.

Chapter Seven

"I've spoken to our solicitor, Sam," Mrs Foster said, "and the hearing is set for tomorrow morning, at the magistrates court."

Sam was getting ready for his walk with Jake.

"Tomorrow morning!" Sam said. "Will they decide tomorrow, whether Jake is guilty or not?"

"I think so," Mrs Foster said.

"And if . . ." Sam paused to take a

breath. He couldn't bear to say what he was thinking.

"If they find Jake guilty," Mrs Foster said, "they will keep him at the court and decide what to do with him."

"You mean, kill him?" Sam said.

"I hope not!" Mrs Foster said, but she knew it would probably be so.

Sam's eyes filled with tears.

Mr and Mrs Foster loved Jake and hated the thought of losing him. But it was Sam who would miss Jake more than anyone. Sam and Jake had a very special friendship. Jake had saved Sam's life and he had given him a reason to enjoy life. Sam had made friends with people through Jake. He couldn't imagine life without him.

Jake listened to the conversation and was very quiet when he and Sam reached the park.

Jake told the other dogs the bad news. Tomorrow was judgment day.

Boris did not hesitate. He quickly told the others that they must put their plan into action now. If things went badly for Jake tomorrow, they would never have another chance. They were to be ready and only move on his signal.

The dogs and their owners were gathered by the entrance to the park. Boris began to bark and at once, Holly, Charles and Boris started to circle round Jake and Sam.

"Stop!" said Mrs Thirkettle. "What are you doing? You're getting us all in a muddle. All the leads are getting tied up together!"

But the dogs carried on. They twisted in and out of one another until all the leads, dogs and owners were completely tangled up.

"What a mess!" said Mr Grant.

Boris warned the dogs to be ready. The owners had to let go of the leads to untangle them and as soon as they did, all the dogs ran off in different directions.

The owners were worried that the dogs were now running loose in the park. They knew this was no longer allowed. What they didn't know was that somebody had seen them and telephoned the police.

"At last!" thought Jake. "I'm free!" and he ran as fast as he could to the ice house. When he reached the entrance, he stopped.

He looked inside for a moment, but it was too dark to see anything. He could smell something though. The same smell as before. The smell that had been all around the dead swan. And this time, it was very strong. The creature, whatever it was, was in the ice house.

Jake listened. It was very quiet but Jake thought he could hear breathing. He hesitated. Suddenly, he didn't feel quite so brave and he wondered if he should risk going into the ice house. Then he heard the sound of Sam, running through the park, trying to catch up with him. It was now or never.

"Here goes!" thought Jake and he went down into the blackness of the ice house.

It was so dark that Jake couldn't see at first. Before his eyes could get used to the gloom, something gave a frightening snarl and grabbed him by the throat.

Jake tried to use his legs to push the creature off but it was too strong.

The creature threw Jake to the floor and sank its teeth into him again. Jake was in terrible pain and he was having trouble breathing.

"Come on," he told himself. "This thing isn't too big for you. Get up." He tried to get to his feet. But the animal kept its grip on him and pushed him back down.

Jake struggled with the creature and managed to loosen its hold. He sank his own sharp teeth into the creature's leg. The sudden pain made the animal angry and it grabbed Jake's neck again and shook him.

Jake was exhausted. This was one fight he couldn't win. The creature was too strong for him.

In the struggle, Jake caught sight of what looked like dead birds in a corner of the ice house. Jake had an idea.

The creature still had hold of Jake but, using all his strength, Jake struggled to his feet. He raised his hackles and growled. He pressed as hard as he could against the animal, pushing his thick, hairy mane into its nose. Finding it couldn't breath, the creature at last let go.

As quickly as he could, Jake grabbed one of the dead birds and ran out of the ice house, hoping that the creature would follow him.

It worked. Angrily, the animal rushed after Jake into the daylight.

Outside the ice house, a crowd of dogs and people had gathered to see what was happening. Among them was a police dog-handler. He had a net with him which was meant for Jake.

He missed Jake but then he saw the creature coming out of the ice house. It was blinded by the daylight for a moment and the policeman threw the net over the animal and tranquillised it with a dart.

"My goodness, what have we here?" he said.

Everyone stared at the creature lying quietly in the net.

"Gracious!" said Mrs Thirkettle. "It's a wolf!" She took a step closer to look at the animal in the net. "I think it's a Timber Wolf," she said. "And if it is, it's very dangerous, especially when it's hungry."

Jake was lying, exhausted, by the ice

house. Sam ran over to him and examined him closely. He had two very nasty bites in his throat and he was shivering.

"We must get you to the vet, Jake. You clever boy. You knew that creature was killing the birds and I think you've probably saved your own life with your bravery," Sam said.

The other dogs gathered round Jake. They were full of admiration for him. No other dog would have dared to take on a wolf. How brave he was.

Jake thanked them. He couldn't have done it without their help. Boris's plan had worked brilliantly.

Boris said that he thought Jake had been magnificent. Boris had seen what wolves could do to other animals in Canada. Now he knew why the smell of the ice house had reminded him of

Canada. Wolves lived wild there, but Boris had never seen one, only the remains of their kills.

Holly looked anxiously at Jake's wounds. He was still trembling.

Jake reassured her that he would be all right and he tried to get up. But he quickly wobbled back down.

"Come on, old boy," Sam said. He picked Jake up and, with a great effort, carried him home.

Chapter Eight

Later that day, Jake returned from the vet. He had stitches in his wounds and some tablets to help him heal.

"He seems remarkably well," the vet had said. "He'll take a day or two to recover from the shock, but he's a fit dog, and it'll take more than a brush with a wolf to finish him off."

It was what would happen at the magistrates court that was still worrying the Fosters and Sam.

Jake was sleeping peacefully in his box, when the telephone rang. Mr Foster answered it.

"Yes. That's right? We are due at the magistrates court tomorrow. Yes," said Mr Foster.

"What's happening? Who is it?" asked Mrs Foster.

"Shush, I can't hear," said Mr Foster. "Oh not you, officer, I was talking to my wife."

Mr Foster listened in silence for quite some time. Mrs Foster and Sam were becoming very impatient to know what was being said.

At last, Mr Foster said, "Really? That's excellent! Well thank you very much, officer. Thank you for all your help. That's very good news." Mr Foster hung up.

"Well? Who was it? What did they

say?" Mrs Foster and Sam said, excitedly.

"It was the police dog-handler who trapped the wolf," Mr Foster said. "He says that they are sure the wolf is responsible for the killings. They are dropping their charges against Jake."

"Does that mean we don't have to go to the magistrates court?" Sam said.

"Yes, it means Jake is a free dog!" Mr Foster said. "The dog-handler said that the wolf was one of Mr Wood's animals. Can you believe it? Mr Wood let him go free some weeks ago. He thought a wolf would be all right living wild."

"Perhaps it would be, with more space to roam around in than the park," Sam said. "But the park is too small for a wolf. And the wolf is too fierce for the park. It was sure to kill the animals. Silly man."

"Well, the police officer said that they think they've found a home for it already.

There's a wildlife park in Scotland where there's a pack of wolves," Mr Foster said. "It's possible that they will take all the animals. At least then they would be kept together."

Jake listened to all of this, from his box. He was safe. What a relief!

In the evening, Jake tottered out into the garden to tell Holly his good news. He was also pleased that the wolf was to be given another chance as well. It was only killing things because it needed to eat.

Holly thought Jake was very generous to the wolf, after all it had done to him. She was impressed.

Over the next few weeks, the police dog-handler called several times to see how Jake was getting on. He liked Jake.

Sam chatted to the policeman and they laughed together about Jake's attempts at agility. Sam thought there must be some dog sport that Jake would be good at.

The policeman thought for a moment. "Is Jake good with a ball?" he asked.

"Brilliant!" Sam said.

"Right. When he's completely better, I think I've got just the thing for him. I'll take you along."

Chapter Nine

One evening, as promised, the policeman arrived to take the Fosters, Sam and Jake along to his training classes.

They walked into a big hall. At the end of the hall, there were some strange looking machines with levers on them and big funnels sticking out of the front.

The machines were filled with balls. When a lever was pressed, a ball would fly out of the funnel. The dogs had to run as fast as possible to the machines, press the lever, catch a ball in their mouths and run back to the start line. The dog that arrived back first with a ball in its mouth was the winner. The game was called flyball.

"Easy!" thought Jake.

"Do you think Jake would like to try?" said the policeman.

"I think he would love it," Mrs Foster said.

Jake lined up at the start, next to another dog. He had learnt what to do, just by watching.

The policeman said "Go!" and the dogs set off. Jake got to his machine first, pushed the lever, caught the ball, and ran back to the start. The other dog hadn't even got the ball yet.

"Simple!" Jake thought.

"Well done!" the policeman said. "Let's see how he does against our champion." And he led a police dog over to the start.

The two dogs lined up. The race started and Jake ran to his machine. He pushed the lever but, instead of just catching the ball, he headed it three times on his nose. He trapped it with his paws

and dribbled it back to the start. Jake still arrived back first and he looked very pleased with himself.

"Tremendous skill," laughed the policeman, "But I'm afraid it doesn't count. The ball has to be in his mouth!"

Sam grinned. "That's Jake!"

"I thought we'd found something he was good at!" sighed Mrs Foster.

The policeman patted Jake's head and smiled.

"You have. I think Jake's very good at being himself!" he laughed.

And Jake had to agree.